For Helen, Claire, & Eoin.
– E.R.L.

For Sandy Suggs (iced tea) and Bernie Coughlan (hippie tea),
and for the Aunties – Anne, Rosie, Laura and Stephanie.
– M.A.S.

Copyright © 2017, Clavis Publishing Inc. New York

Visit us on the Web at www.clavisbooks.com.

A *Cup of Tea?* written by Eric La Branche and illustrated by Margaret Anne Suggs

ISBN 978-1-60537-281-5

This book was printed in July 2017 at Publikum d.o.o., Slavka Rodica 6, Belgrade, Serbia.

First Edition
10 9 8 7 6 5 4 3 2 1

A Cup of Tea?

Eric La Branche &
Margaret Anne Suggs

Clavis

NEW YORK

When Mommy got home from work today,
she was "oh, so tired," too weary play.
I had hoped she would go on a bug hunt with me,
but she just wanted to relax "with a nice cup of tea."

Perhaps she could play after she rested a spell,
but just then I heard the front door bell.
It was Aunt Margaret, full of kisses and hugs.
I'd rather have Mommy help me search for some bugs.

While I searched alone for spiders and flies,
Aunt Margaret and Mommy drank tea and ate pies.
I invited them both to explore with me.
Their answer? "Give us a minute to finish our tea."

Finally Aunt Margaret was saying goodbye...
She had one more large cookie and a bite of mince pie.
Now Mommy could have some fun time with me;
she could not possibly drink any more tea.

As Mommy and Aunt Margaret hugged at the door,
I had an idea; we'll draw a dinosaur!
I dashed to the playroom to get art supplies,
but I heard a hello amid all the goodbyes.

Now, who on earth could this possibly be?
It was time for Mommy to spend time with me!
I stormed into the room feeling rather berserk,
but was relieved to see Daddy just home from work.

Now all three of us could draw a huge dinosaur,
with enormous claws and great giant ROAR!
But Daddy was weary and as he kissed Mom and me.
He asked if he could just "have a nice cup of tea."

Once again my adventures were undone by the kettle!
It gets so much use, now I know why it's metal.
I just wanted to have a little bit of fun
before it's bedtime and the whole day is done.

I knew Mom and Dad would drink tea later tonight.
So I came up with a plan that might work out right,
It's a little bit sneaky but I'm definitely a smarty:
I'll invite them both to a fancy tea party.

So while Daddy showered and Mommy did chores,
  I prepared the treats behind closed kitchen doors.
  I put stacks of cakes on a gold serving plate,
    though not quite as many as Aunt Margaret ate.

Around the table sat my favorite teddies,
   and I decorated it all with sprinkled confetti.
The setting was really such a glorious sight.
"My Tea Party" would be the most perfect night.

With no time to waste, Mom and Dad were invited.
When they entered the room they were very excited.
But just then it suddenly occurred to me
that I had forgotten a fresh pot of tea!

My tea party was ruined and I wanted to cry.
I wanted to moan; I wanted to sigh.
I planned the whole party and now it wouldn't be.
You can't have a tea party with treats but no tea!

But Mommy smiled brightly and held me so close,
while Daddy laughed fondly and then blew my nose.
Instead of having the usual cup of tea,
they said that they'd rather have a special "cup of me"!

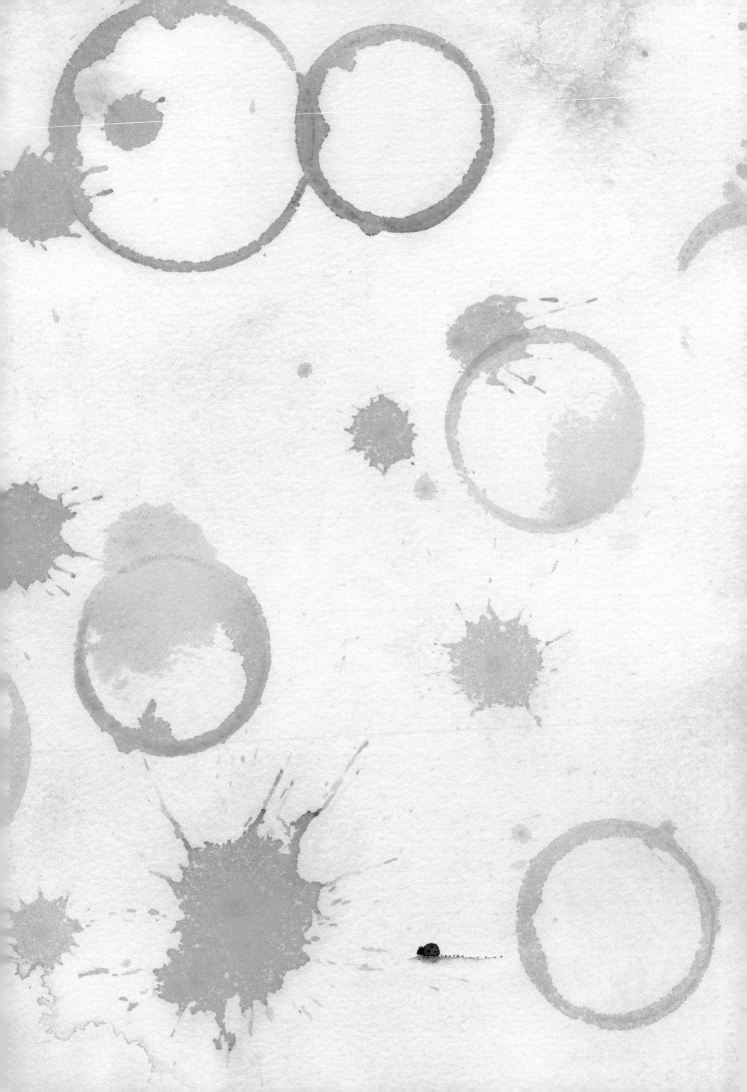